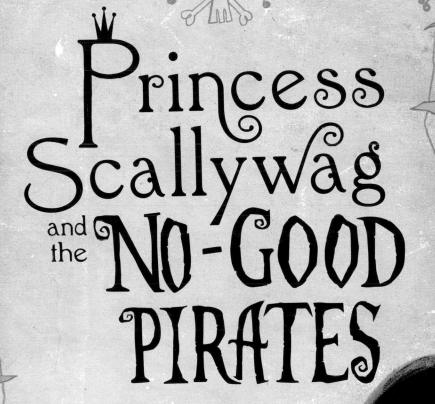

Princess Scallywag and the No-GOOD PIRATES

—

MARK SPERRING
CLAIRE POWELL

For Jeanetté, with thanks for all those Cornish holidays.
- M. S.

For Mum, who taught me not to be fooled by no-good pirates!
- C. P.

First published in paperback in Great Britain by HarperCollins *Children's Books* in 2019

1 3 5 7 9 10 8 6 4 2

ISBN: 978-00-0-821299-5

HarperCollins *Children's Books* is a division of HarperCollins *Publishers* Ltd.

Text copyright © Mark Sperring 2019
Illustrations copyright © Claire Powell 2019

Visit our website at: www.harpercollins.co.uk

Printed in China

Princess Scallywag and the No-Good Pirates

MARK SPERRING

illustrated by

CLAIRE POWELL

HarperCollins *Children's Books*

One day Princess Scallywag and the Queen were out on the *royal yacht*, enjoying the fresh sea air, when they noticed two little stowaways peering sweetly from the royal hamper …

ribbit

"It's always nice to receive unexpected visitors!" declared the Queen, offering them each a sandwich,

BUT ...

before those froggy stowaways could take a single bite, the royal yacht gave a sudden **JOLT** and some far less welcome guests jumped aboard ...

And they waved their swords in the most ALARMING way!

"I'm afraid we mean to take you prisoner and turn you into galley slaves!" their Captain said with a **dastardly** grin.

"Well!" said the Queen. "That won't do at all. Neither myself nor my daughter, Princess Scallywag, are very good in the kitchen and I fear we will **poison** the lot of you!"

"Poison, you say?" said the Captain, quite taken aback.

"Yes, **POISON**!" continued the Queen.

"We once baked a cake for a royal picnic and one poor fellow took one bite, broke out in **purple spots** …

THEN …

DROPPED DOWN DEAD!"

THUD!

"It's because we *always* forget to wash our hands before cooking!" grinned Princess Scallywag, scratching her behind.

"Regrettably, it often proves **FATAL**," sighed the Queen, pretending to pick her nose.

"Well," said the Captain, "perhaps that's not such a good idea after all. Maybe you'd be better suited to scrubbing the decks ..."

"Hmmm," said the Queen, "my only concern is tripping hazards ... As you already know we *are* a forgetful pair and, although we'd scrub the decks very well, we'd **DEFINITELY** forget to pick up our buckets after we'd finished.

Sooner or later,
one, if not all of you, would …

trip over those forgotten pails

and fall overboard

AND DROWN!"

sPLOOSH!

"If you don't want to drown, perhaps you should find us another job," suggested Princess Scallywag helpfully.

The Captain thought … and thought …

but couldn't think
of a **single one** …

"Maybe it's better if we just **toss you into the sea**?" He shrugged, and the other pirates raised their swords and gave a **HEARTY** cheer!

"OOH-ARRR!'

"TIME TO ...

WALK THE PLANK!"

"Hold on a minute!" said the Queen.
"Do you know what job we'd be *really* good at?"

The Captain shook his head ...

"SWORD-CARRYING

PIRATES

– like you!" beamed the Queen.

"Oh yes!!!" said Princess Scallywag.

"No one is more **VILLAINOUS** or **TREACHEROUS** than us ...

Once we climbed a beanstalk and lulled a *bad-tempered* **GIANT** to sleep with a soothing song and an entire bottle of sleeping potion."

Z Z Z Z Z Z Z Z Z Z Z Z Z

Sleeping Potion

"When he **finally** awoke, he discovered we'd helped ourselves to a big slice of apple pie, a few **DELICIOUS** cookics and a **WHOLE DUNGEON** full of gold coins!"

KA-CHING!

The three pirates seemed to mull this over for a moment ...

"I know what you're thinking," said the Queen, "that we'd probably betray you the first chance we got, too ... but the truth is we've *already* proven our loyalty TWICE today ..."

"You have?!" said the Captain, looking confused.

"Of course!" sighed Princess Scallywag, thinking that the Captain was a **COMPLETE NINCOMPOOP**. "Don't you remember? First we saved you from possible food *poisoning* ..."

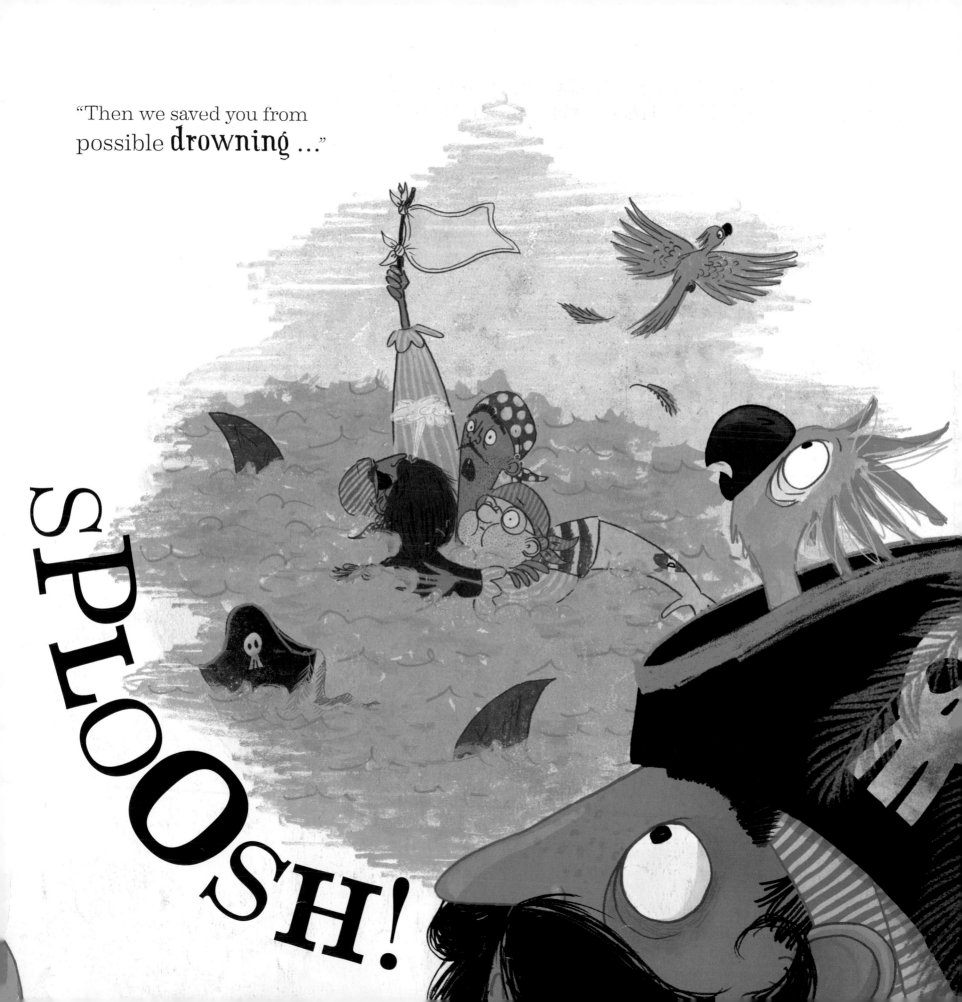

"Then we saved you from possible **drowning** ..."

SPLOOSH!

The Captain said it was indeed true and thanked them for their *loyal* support thus far. Then he handed them each a sword and some pirate accessories …

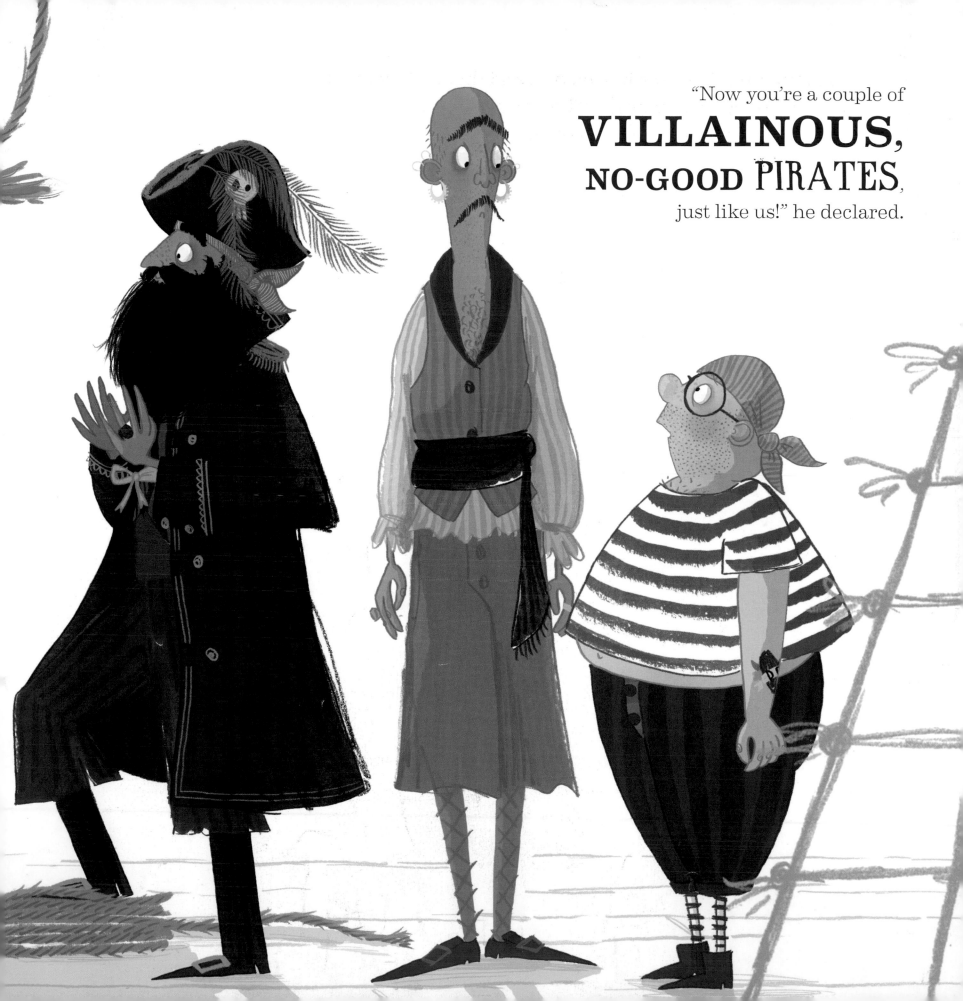

"Now you're a couple of **VILLAINOUS, NO-GOOD PIRATES**, just like us!" he declared.

"Indeed we arrrrrrr!" grinned the new recruits.
And, to prove it, Princess Scallywag
jumped high into the
air and ...

SWOOSH!

... cut down the sail!

And the Queen tied a quick and *pretty bow*!

"What are you going to do with us?" came the muffled cry of the captured Captain. "Are you going to turn us into galley slaves or make us walk **the plank**?"

"Nothing so **terrible** as THAT," said Princess Scallywag.

"In fact, we're going to leave you right here on the *royal yacht* and when you *finally* manage to untie yourselves I suggest you sail away so we **NEVER** BUMP INTO YOU AGAIN!"

"But what about you?" asked the Captain. "How will you get back to shore?"

"We're taking **your** boat of course!" said the Queen.

"Yes," grinned Princess Scallywag, "with its JOLLY ROGER FLAG it's *much* more suited to our

SCALLYWAG WAYS!"

Then, with a loud and *hearty* cheer ...

"OOH-ARRR!"

...off they sailed ...

leaving those **NO-GOOD**
and **VILLAINOUS** PIRATES
far, far behind.